F*CK AND FALL IN LOVE

NICOLE FALLS

Silent N Publishing

Acknowledgments

ch, cj, dw, sr: thanks for reading & providing feedback
ab,sl: thanks for all of the ridiculousness
nyc: thanks for the inspiration

Q1: APRIL

It started with a trip to a rooftop bar. Actually, it all started with a command from my boss. I was sent out of town for business, a trip deemed necessary by my boss but bequeathed unto me because Robyn couldn't miss her goddaughter's debut as Elsa the Snow Queen in a local middle school production of Frozen. So, I was the one sent out East to meet with leadership at our parent company. Hour after hour of boring meetings that I smiled and bullshitted my way through for three days. *Extend your trip through the weekend, take in some of the sights*, my boss said. *The company will cover the expenses of hotel and flight, so why not take advantage*? she further insisted. So, I did. Even invited one of my good girlfriends, Ebonée to take the train up from DC so we could party in the City. But we weren't the young whipper snappers we once were, and mommy duties called for Eb, so it was just me...myself and I for this adventure.

First, there was dinner. The hotel in which I was staying housed a renowned celebrity chef owned and operated restaurant that I'd been wanting to try for quite some time. I was fortunate enough to snag a table because I went down at the right time. I'd been sitting—pretending to look at the menu to figure out what I was going to eat despite having obsessed over it before I stepped foot in the place. I knew exactly what I wanted already—when I felt the eerie sensation of being watched. Covertly, I let my eyes flit about the restaurant trying to find the source but there was no one visible to me that seemed to be paying me any extraordinary attention. Shaking off the feeling, I returned to my fake perusal of the menu until my waitress appeared to take my order. She was the overly perky, way too glad to have her job, taking entirely too long to tell me the specials type—my absolute favorite, of course. I cut her spiel short, informing her that I knew what I wanted to order for not only dinner, but dessert as well. I made sure that although I was curt, my tone remained polite as I conveyed my desires to her, not wanting to earn any ill will with anyone who had the power to fuck over my food. I was just all small talked out after having been in meeting after meeting after meeting this afternoon.

Yuliya, my waitress, who was way more in tune with the human condition than I'd previously given her credit, quickly picked up on my mood as she strutted away to put my meal order in. After about ninety seconds, she returned with a glass of red wine. I peered up at her curious because I hadn't asked for anything more to drink than room temperature water and a straw.

"I didn't—" I started but was quickly interrupted by Yuliya.

"This was sent over by the gentleman seated at the end of the bar. Said you looked like you could use it," she said, "I told him that you probably weren't going to accept it, but he wouldn't take no for an answer. It's a Spanish red blend—Tempranillo, Graciano and Garnacha. Say the word and I'll take it back to the bar."

I looked over to see a fine brotha seated at the

end of the bar with smooth ebony skin, neatly trimmed beard and mustache, and shiny bald head. Our eyes met briefly, and he lifted the glass of brown liquor he'd been clutching in salute. Involuntarily, the left side of my mouth lifted in a smirk—my only gesture of acknowledgement.

"You can leave it, Yuliya," I replied, smoothly, "and tell the gentleman his overture is appreciated."

"Will do," she trilled, setting the glass down before retreating from the table.

I fully expected that once she delivered that message Mister Tall Fine and Delicious would undoubtedly make his way over to me to occupy the seat on the other side of my small table, but that's what I got for assuming. He continued to sit at the bar and finish his drink, then left the area altogether with no further acknowledgement of me beyond that glass of wine. Which was super delicious by the way! How he knew I was a dry red kind of girl was beyond me, but I was definitely thankful for the assist. I'd been unable to make a decision on my own which is why I'd ended up with water. Soon my meal arrived, short rib risotto that was cooked to perfection and I made love to every delectable morsel with my mouth. I ended up canceling my dessert order, so stuffed from my dinner. I settled up with Yuliya and slowly made my way out of the restaurant and over to the elevators up to my room. Since Eb had abandoned me, I'd be calling it a night early.

I got up to my room, showered, moisturized and changed into my night shirt, crawling into bed with the remote, hoping to find something streaming to binge. My room was outfitted with a Smart TV that I could use to log into Netflix, Hulu and other streaming services to indulge in hours of mindless television to my heart's content. I quickly found a series that Eb had told me about and started the first episode. I ended up restarting the episode a few times because I couldn't seem to actually stay focused on what was going on. I was restless and listless, going back and forth between scrolling social media mindlessly and trying to give a damn about the show currently on the screen. I gave up on the show after the third restart—getting out of bed, throwing on a cute little dress and making my way to the rooftop terrace bar that was situated on the top floor of the hotel. The weather wasn't exactly right to frequent this type of establishment, but it was mostly enclosed, with a few brave souls braving the slight chill in the air to take in beautiful views of the city that were definitely Instagram—*with the caption hashtag no filter*—worthy. I posted up at the tiny bar that was in the center of the room, snagging the last stool at the corner end of it. The bartender, an adorable tiny sprite of a woman, signaled to me that she'd be with me shortly as she finished pouring a couple drafts for a couple who stood there waiting.

Once again, that eerie feeling of being watched came over me, but I shook it off.

"What can I get you, doll?" the bartender asked brightly, grinning broadly at me and looking slightly unhinged.

"Whatever's the best drink you make...I'll have that," I replied.

It was a calculated risk. People tended to do their best when showing off. I didn't do it often, but in establishments where I thought they held their employees to a certain standard I made it bartender's choice. It usually worked in my favor because the bartender was composing a drink to impress so I knew it would be delicious.

"Anything you don't drink?" the bartender asked.

I shook my head slowly.

"Okay, I got you," she squeaked before turning on a heel and heading to the middle of the bar where most of her mixology equipment was. A few minutes of her pouring shots and tinctures into a shaker passed before she floated back over to me, serving my drink with a flourish.

"This," she said as she pulled a coaster for the drink to rest upon, "is the truth serum. A couple of these and you'll be unable to stop yourself from blabbing your truths all over the place."

"I'll be sure to have just one," I laughed, "I don't need my business in the streets of a town that ain't even mine."

"What brings you in town?"

"Hold tight, stranger danger, I don't even know your name and now you want my life story. Typical barkeep," I giggled.

She wiped her hands on a small towel behind the bar before extending her left one in my direction, "Abril, nice to meet ya!"

I returned her enthusiastic handshake and couldn't help cracking on her name, "April in Spanish?"

"Girl, my mama thought she was being creative. Only this name has led to a lifetime of people calling me April any damn way."

"Everyone in this place has such unique names," I remarked, "First Yuliya downstairs now you up here... is that a prerequisite for a job in this hotel? I'd never get a job here in that case, I'm just plain ass Jane."

"Oop! Looks like the truth serum is already working," Abril laughed, "Let me grab you a glass of water. Let me know if you need anything else."

"Thanks, Spanish April," I called after her, bobbing my head to the music playing in the background that had seemed to get a bit louder since I'd taken a couple sips of my drink.

My drink, which was damn delicious by the way. *Bartender roulette paid off in my favor tonight*, I thought. Swiveling on the barstool I took in the scene around me. The place was moderately crowded with a mix of folks who looked like they were holdovers from the happy hour set and others who were just getting their nights started. Everyone was smartly dressed, attired in various ways that made it easy for me to partake in my favorite pastime of making up stories about strangers. I usually preferred to do this when accompanied because sharing the stories was part of the fun of the pastime. I grew annoyed at once again being out dolo and turned around to my phone that was perched on the bar to shoot off a text to Eb.

In that rooftop bar we were coveting when these plans were made, sad my bestie isn't here to hear about the tales of these folks in here. We've got some doozies.

She should have been here, honestly, but her asswipe of an ex just happened to have forgotten that it was his weekend to have the kids. So, to make up for their weak ass father, Eb planned a weekend of activity to keep their minds off the fact that their dad was useless beyond the hefty monthly check he wrote to help supplement their care.

You need to focus that energy onto seeing if one of these strangers you're profiling is single and get some out of town dick, beloved. -Eb the Great

Chill, Eb. I fired back immediately.

Ain't nobody tryna end up with stranger danger dick.

Clear out the cobwebs, sis. You deserve. – Eb the Great

She was right...I did deserve. It had been entirely too long since I'd felt or seen a warm dick in person, but I wasn't fucking a stranger just for the hell of it. And even if that was something that I was open to? Pickings were slim as hell in this place. The crowd was mostly groups of women, the occasional man sprinkled in here and there. None of them looking remotely interesting to me nor interested in me. I texted a little bit more with Eb before flagging down Spanish April for a refill.

"You sure?" she asked.

I nodded emphatically, "I've just got a short elevator ride to get through, so I can't get into too much trouble."

"Be careful what you wish for, Plain Jane," she replied ominously, before breaking into high pitched giggles.

I finished off the last sip of my first drink just as Abril placed the second one in front of me. I grabbed it up quickly, taking a greedy sip. The heat of the alcohol seemed to warm me much more intensely this go around, sending prickly sensations of energy throughout my body. Suddenly, the music switched to one of my favorite songs and I was overcome with the need to get up and dance. Gathering my small clutch, I threw my phone in there, then slipped it onto my wrist before grabbing my drink and heading to the makeshift dancefloor area in the center of the space. It was completely empty, but the truth serum apparently contained courage as well because I was unbothered as I sipped and got my groove on, rapping along to the old ass Lil Kim song that played.

Apparently, all everyone else was waiting on was one fool to get the party going because before long, most of the people who were in the bar were crowded onto the dancefloor, dancing and singing along with the set that the DJ had slid into, which was full of late 90s and early 2000s hip-hop. It took me back to my days of undergrad, when my girls and I stayed in the clubs and bars from Wednesday night through Sunday. It was a miracle that I'd managed to graduate not only on time, but summa cum laude. After partying my ass off for a couple more hours, with a couple more truth serums, I was reminded that this was not undergrad as a sudden tiredness swept over me in a wave. I went to cash out with Spanish April and grab a bottle of water for the elevator ride when my gaze collided with a smoldering, obsidian one.

"It's you..." I breathed out, as if he could hear me despite him being halfway across a room that was booming with music from the DJ.

The fine, wine sending brotha from the restaurant earlier was standing near the exit, and still happened to be there after I had settled my bill and walked over to the elevator and waited for to arrive. As a group of people came up the stairs and he checked their IDs, and instantly I felt a bit deflated. I'd chalked his presence up to stalling until I arrive so that he could finally say something. I could still feel his gaze on me, but he said nothing. It was unnerving yet thrilling. The attraction between us crackled in the air. Just being in this man's presence had my pussy weeping. Something about him instantly made me imagine how he'd look with that shiny bald head between my thighs or with my feet pressed into his shoulders as he piped me down with rapid-fire, pounding, breathtaking strokes. *Hell, maybe Eb's idea of stranger danger dick wasn't such a bad idea* I thought before giggling to myself. I shook my head trying to rid myself of the lust-filled thoughts that were playing in full-color HD in my imagination right now. Where in the hell is that elevator?

"The elevator always takes forever," he spoke in a deep, rolling tone.

I shifted, turning in his direction.

"Did...I say that outloud?" I asked.

"Mmmmhmm."

That low murmuring answer brought the lusty thoughts right on back as I saw myself riding him, reverse cowgirl, as he murmured his agreement when I asked him if my pussy felt good to him. I shook my head once again, then tilted it in his direction.

"What's your name?" I asked.

"Nigel. And yours?"

I moved closer to where he stood, closing the space between us.

"Jane. Nice to meet you," I replied holding out my hand.

He captured it immediately, raising it to his mouth for a brief kiss, "Believe me, sweetheart, the pleasure is all mine."

The elevator dinged and a group of folks came off. Nigel commenced to doing his job, but not before calling out to me, "You have a good night, Ms. Jane."

"You too, Nigel," I called out just as the elevator doors shut, so I was unsure he even heard me.

The smallest part of me wanted to press the door open to make sure he heard me and also invite him down to room 1882 after he got off work, but the larger part of me tamped down that crazy talk and took my ass back down to the eighteenth floor, washed my face, brushed my teeth, put on my bonnet and changed into my PJs before crashing onto the bed looking like a human starfish.

The next morning, I woke up and decided to take the day to be a tourist. I rode double decker buses, ferries, trains. I went up in some very tall buildings, capturing views of this city from many different angles. Ones I'd never even taken the time out to acknowledge or enjoy any other time I'd been here in the city. I wanted to make the most of this day because I had a stupid early flight out in the morning. For some reason, probably frugality even thought this trip was being expensed, I'd booked a very early morning flight home. So, my plan was to be on the go all day today so I could crash early because I needed to be in a Lyft by 3:45am at the latest to make it to the airport on time for my flight.

However, even after traipsing all over this city for nearly ten hours I was still keyed up. I came back to my room, showered and hoped that would bring me down but I was still too wired. Thinking about the great night's sleep I got after drinking those Truth Serums—without hangover, despite overindulging—I decided to make my way up to the terrace bar once again for a drink. And if I was being completely honest, the drink wasn't the only thing driving me toward the terrace. My brain had bombarded me with imagery of Nigel's handsome ass face all throughout the previous night, causing me to awaken with a stark feeling of disappointment to wake up to my own hands between my legs, furiously sending me careening headfirst into orgasm.

So, I slipped on a little black dress, fixed my face, and carried my ass up the elevator to the thirty-sixth floor where the terrace bar was situated. It took a minute for an elevator that wasn't ridiculously crowded to make a stop at my floor. As I rode up with a handful of other folks, my nerves rattled in the pit of my stomach. If Nigel was here, what would I say? Would he even remember me? I'm sure he meets plenty of people on a daily basis working here and doesn't remember every random female that strikes up a conversation with him while waiting for the elevator. The ding of the elevator signaled our arrival and as soon as the doors opened, a familiar wave of heat washed over me. He was definitely here, dressed in all black from head to toe, he checked the IDs of my elevator pals, as I purposefully made it so I'd be the last person to enter in this wave of people.

Wordlessly I held out my ID.

"You came back," Nigel rumbled, a slight grin on his face.

"Who can say no to Spanish April's Truth Serum?" I tossed out lightly, "Is she working tonight?"

Nigel nodded, "Yep, we're both here all night."

"Cool," I replied, instantly feeling stupid after I'd

uttered the one word, "I'm just gonna..." I gestured with my hands toward the bar.

"You enjoy your night, Ms. Jane," Nigel called after me.

I barely heard him over the thumping bass of the music playing. The vibe was distinctively different tonight, way clubbier than it had been last night. I made my way over to the bar, slinking through gatherings of people to the end of the bar where Abril was working.

"PJ!" she yelled out, waving at me.

I pointed to myself.

She nodded, waving me closer, "PJ! Girl you had it crackin' in here last night!"

"Are you sure you mean me?"

"Jane, right? You don't have a twin, do you?"

I shook my head, apparently remembering less of the night than what actually happened. But no, Abril was just talking about me singing and dancing all around like I didn't have a care in the world. I ordered a Truth Serum and a water, hoping some space would free up so I could nurse my drink at the bar, but it was hella packed. I wound up snagging a piece of wall space not too far from the DJ. It didn't take long before I'd made my way to the dance floor, with a fresh drink in hand. Grooving until I felt my body finally coming down from its earlier buzz, so I settled up with Abril and headed to the elevators. I pressed the button and stood waiting, all the while feeling singed by Nigel's gaze. *There he goes with that staring but not saying shit thing again. I should say somethin. But what...* I thought before sauntering over in his direction to stand in front of him.

"You know, I never got to properly thank you?" I said, peering up at him.

He had me dwarfed by nearly a foot, so it hurt my neck a little to keep it craned up at him, making direct eye contact.

"For?" he replied, looking puzzled.

"My wine? At the restaurant. That was you, right?"

He chuckled, biting his lower lip, "Yeah... Yuliya wasn't exactly supposed to put my business out there. I just saw you sitting there, fine as all hell, but clearly stressed. I took a chance on my choice, but just wanted to see that beautiful smile that graced your face after you took that first sip. I felt called by a higher power to be the one to make you smile that day."

It was like those words flipped a switch in me, my previous shyness completely evaporated as I damn near purred, "What time are you off tonight? I owe you a proper thank you."

"We're open until two tonight," Nigel replied smoothly.

"Oh yeah," I said, sliding even closer to Nigel as I opened my clutch, pulling out my spare room key and sliding it into the front pocket on the slacks that he wore. As my hand retreated, it brushed against *not-solittle* Nigel and I hoped like hell I wasn't shooting this shot to get it batted down. I'd opened my mouth to tell him my room number when the elevator dinged. I backed toward the elevator, keeping Nigel's gaze ensnared in mine, "Eighteen eighty-two if you want that thank you."

As soon as the elevator doors closed, a small part of me was immediately stricken with regret. What the hell was I doing, inviting a perfect stranger into my hotel room that I didn't know from a can of paint? Who cared that he worked for this hotel? There was no telling if he was a crazy psycho serial killer and I'd just set myself up to become his next victim! The larger, more adventurous part of me was completely satisfied and won over. I had about two hours before Nigel would be off work and possibly at my room, so I decided to take a quick cat nap, get up and freshen up so I'd be ready for whatever, whether he showed or not.

Fifteen minutes after two am, I heard the lock to my room's door disengaging, which made me sit up from my reclined place in bed. I popped out of bed just as Nigel crossed the threshold of the door.

"Whassup?" he asked, licking that damn lower lip again.

"Hi," I said, shyly, like I wasn't the one who invited this man down to my room to give me a dick transfusion.

Nigel engaged the deadbolt on the room door then headed toward me with his jacket draped over his arm and a cup filled with some undetermined brown liquor and a couple cherries in it. He dropped the jacket on the little bench that rested at the end of the bed and walked right up on me. He said nothing as he looked down at my attire, then took a slow sip of his drink. The simple sleep dress I wore seemed inadequate when I came back to my room to weigh my options of what I should or should not be wearing if he showed. The fire in his eyes as he gazed at me now, however, made me feel silly for my earlier freak out. He sipped and stared a little too long for my liking, as I squirmed under his perusal.

"What are you drinking?" I asked.

"You wanna taste?" he replied.

I shook my head, "I have to get up early in the... well, actually I should be getting up right about now."

"I didn't ask if you wanted a sip, I asked if you wanted a taste," Nigel replied, leaning down to press a soft, fleeting kiss against my lips.

He continued to tease me with those barely there kisses until I put my hands behind his neck and deepened the contact, immediately opening my mouth for his tongue to slide in and give me a taste of whatever he was drinking. I wasn't too much a brown liquor connoisseur, they all tasted like a burning mess to me.

Whatever it was had a kick of spice as our tongues tangled and dueled with one another. Nigel placed his drink down on the end table next to the bed before hands moved down to grip my ass. I yelped as he lifted me to straddle his waist in one easy movement, not breaking our kiss at all as he maneuvered us. He placed me onto the bed, but remained standing as he removed his shirt, the tee beneath it and his belt. Then he leaned down to connect our mouths again. Nigel's kisses moved from my mouth to my neck as he played with the spaghetti straps of the sleep dress I was wearing. Slipping the straps down my shoulders one by one, Nigel exposed my breasts to his view, grinning broadly as the nipples immediately hardened from his penetrative stare alone. His hands slid up my sides until he was palming a breast in each hand, my erect nipples abrading against his palms. I hissed a curse as he used his fingers to pluck and pull at my nipples, stimulating me to fever pitch once his kisses wandered from my neck further south. At the feel of Nigel's wet mouth suckling at my breast, I moaned aloud. He went back and forth using his mouth and hands to stimulate me, bringing me damn near to orgasm solely with nipple play.

He removed my sleep dress entirely, leaving me laying before him in just my panties. I felt self-conscious under his perusal, wondering if he was counting all of my imperfections that I could name off without a second thought, but that was short lived as he removed his pants leaving him clad in just a pair of tight black boxer briefs. The oversized bulge in his underwear made my earlier feelings of insecurity feel silly as there was zero doubt that this man liked what he was seeing very much. Nigel nudged me to move back on the bed some, as he stalked over me caging me in with his arms and legs. He leaned down applying those teasing kisses to my lips again before I looped my arms around his neck forcing deeper contact and for him to completely cover me with his body. We made out and hunched with our underwear on like novices before Nigel removed my panties and treated me to some of the best head that I'd ever experienced in all the years I'd been letting guys eat me out. His mouth seemed to be all over my lower lips as he licked, sucked, lapped, and fucked me with his tongue.

It didn't take long after the first touch of his mouth to my pussy for my legs to begin shaking signaling that I was close to release. I tried moving back, escaping his rapacious tongue, but Nigel locked an arm around my thigh, securely holding me in place as he went after me with his mouth, tongue darting about as if it was seeking a sweetness that could only be found between my thighs. I came with a sharp curse, the word slicing through the air that had been previously peppered with the sounds of mine and Nigel's moans alternately. Instead of letting up since I was cumming, that caused Nigel to go even harder, his tongue moving as if revved by a power motor, sending my ecstasy to an even higher level. I rapped on the top of his head, beating insistently but he refused to relent. Apparently, the cure to whatever ailed him was in the depths of my pussy and he refused to give up until he consumed every last drop of me.

"Ni...I...cannaaaaaa...plea...oh God oh God oh God oh God...Jesus I'm...whew, shit!" I exclaimed with a hard slap to the top of his head as my back bowed in pleasure once again. This time he let me come down from the orgasm completely and I said, "You fuckin' play too much!"

Nigel chuckled against my sensitive skin and replied, "Believe me sweetheart I definitely wasn't playing. This is playing." He said that as he inserted a first, then a second finger into my slickened flesh. I moaned at the penetration and he murmured, "So fuckin' tight. When's the last time this pussy been fucked, baby?"

I was initially jarred, but quickly turned on by the question. Before I could answer her continued, "This pussy ain't been played in for a while huh? Why have you been starving her? Pussy this good deserves to be sucked and fucked as often as possible."

I grew impossibly wetter at those words and Nigel withdrew his fingers from inside of me, tucking them in the waistband of his underwear to pull them down. And out dropped a whole lot of dick. Before I knew it, I had reached out and grabbed it, marveling over the fact that I needed two hands to hold it completely and he wasn't even fully hard. *Sheesh, dassalotta dick*, I thought.

Nigel's chuckle in response let me know that thought hadn't exactly just been inside my head. I didn't even have the wherewithal to be embarrassed because I was too enthralled with his dick. I let go of it briefly, licked both of my palms, then continued stroking it. Nigel's eyes closed as I hit a pace that must've felt too good to him as he groaned and pistoned his hips into my hands. Before it got too good to him, however, Nigel removed my hands from his dick, positioning the tip of it at the entrance of my lower lips before I pushed back alarmed.

"Wrap that pickle up, jack!" I snapped.

Nigel shook his head, blinked and looked at me before laughing, 'Wrap that pickle up? Yo what in the country hell was that?"

"I said what I meant," I laughed, "We need protection."

He grabbed his wallet from his pants, retrieved a few condoms that he threw onto the nightstand, and then slid one on before moving me back into the position he wanted me in. As his body covered mine, he slowly slid into my depths, groaning when he was fully seated.

"I'm about to stretch this shit out, baby girl. You ready to get stretched out?"

My reply was nothing but a garbled moan as I adjusted to his size. He was still for a couple beats, allowing my body to adjust before he retreated with a slow stroking rhythm that drove me crazy and had me crying out for him to fuck me faster and harder. He kept on with those painfully slow strokes as I cried out in passion, sounding like I was in a damn porno with all of the panting, screaming and cursing that I was doing. By the time Nigel decided to pick up the pace, my voice was scratchy from the overuse of my vocal chords as I screamed out adulations and admonishments to Nigel, giving him total control of my body. He pounded into me mercilessly, my loud, sharp cries fading into an open-mouthed hum as I spasmed, cumming in waves of bliss that rocked me from the tip top of my head through the soles of my feet. I vaguely registered that Nigel was still moving, and it wasn't much longer after I'd succumbed to bliss that Nigel came too, driving into me with a force that almost had me thinking that our bodies were irrevocably fused together.

After a few moments, Nigel retreated from my body, going into the bathroom to dispose of the condom. I laid splayed out on the bed, helpless, boneless. I heard water running and assumed that he was cleaning himself up and about to get out of here. Instead, Nigel walked back into the room carrying a warm soapy towel that he used to clean me up before he collapsed onto the bed beside me. I saw his eyes start to drift close and I nudged him, "Hey...don't fall asleep, I've gotta get outta here soon."

"Say what?" Nigel replied.

"Yep, I have a flight to catch in about three hours. So, you can't fall asleep now," I said, "because I can't go to sleep. So, I guess we'll just have to come up with something to help waste some time."

I leaned forward to press a kiss to his mouth and we lazily made out, hands exploring each other's bodies and getting acquainted. Soon that easy exploration gave way to more insistent and intentional pathways being taken with our hands running along the landscape of each other's bodies with purpose. Lingering touches to incite a moan here, deeper caresses to draw forth a groan there. We were content rounding every base but home until I slid on top of Nigel, grinding my pussy along his renewed erection, wetting up his shaft with my juices. I quickly grabbed one of those condoms from the nightstand and sheathed him so I could ride him into oblivion. But my body didn't get my mind's command because as soon as he was fully embedded within my walls, I began to move my hips in slow, winding circles that eventually gave way to a carefully modulated rolling of my hips.

Nigel's hands at my waist guided my movement, dictating the tempo of our connection as he sat up slightly to bring our mouths together once again. As we kissed, his hands moved from the grip that had settled upon my hips to palming an ass cheek in each hand and he drove his hips upward, driving into me with purpose. Each deep stroke robbed me of the ability to think clearly let alone vocalize an answer when he disconnected our mouths to ask if this was good for me. My only response was a high-pitched scream as he flipped us over and settled between my thighs, still delivering powerful strokes that were driving me completely out of my mind. With my both of my legs hooked over his shoulders, Nigel slowed the tempo once again, retreating then reentering my walls unhurriedly. The combination of those deep, slow strokes and his thumb on my clit was too much and I was cumming once again, hurtling headfirst into the throes of ecstasy panting and screaming for him to never stop doing what he was doing because it felt too good.

"Fuck," Nigel groaned harshly before going over the edge himself, shuddering through release and collapsing onto me. My mouth instantly curved into a smile, finding comfort in the feel of his warm body resting upon me fully. After less than thirty seconds he slid off of me, lying right beside me, hooking an arm around my waist as his fingers traced tiny abstract shapes along my side. We laid there for a few minutes, completely silent until I turned my head to look at the clock on one of the nightstands, then tapped him on the shoulder.

"Okay, now you really gotta go," I giggled.

"Do I?" he asked, trailing nibbling kisses along my neck.

My body's reaction contradicted the shuddering yes that I let out as he zeroed in on a particularly sensitive part of my neck.

"I...shit...I've gotta get to...mmmm...the airport soon," I breathed out.

"So, you just gon use me for my body and discard me, huh? Damn cold world," Nigel said, lightly pressing his lips against mine.

I giggled and slapped his shoulder, "Shut up! Besides, you know you loved every minute of it."

"That I did indeed," he murmured before standing from the bed and stretching.

His beautiful dick was still semi-hard, which almost made me reconsider this early flight and paying the change fees to hop back up on that thang and ride it like a motorbike, but I had things that I needed to get back to at home, so my fun was over. Nigel ambled into the bathroom and I heard sounds of running water for a few minutes before he returned half dressed. I sat up and watched him put on the rest of his things silently. He sipped the last of the liquor in his cup before leaning down toward the bed, his arms resting on either side of me caging me in.

"So, this was fun..." I offered for lack of anything better to say.

We both laughed at that awkward ass ice breaker before he leaned even further to kiss me once again. Just his kisses and soft caresses of my body had me revved up once again, so I groaned in protest when he pulled away once again.

"Safe travels, Miss Jane," Nigel said before grabbing his jacket and walking toward the door.

"Hey!' I called out just before he crossed the door's threshold, "Was that a proper enough thank you?"

He chuckled, "Yeah...and...you're welcome."

Q2: JULY

I tolerated this place on most days, getting by with doing just enough above average to make it seem like I actually enjoyed the work and felt nurtured and fulfilled. I was over exaggerating, I loved my job, honestly. I'd worked very hard to attain this position without the help or aid of others. I came in here and worked my ass off every day. That is why I was singled out by my boss to go to our quarterly corporate meetings which led to me impressing *somebody* with a three lettered title who was in charge of some thing or another at corporate. And because I was *so impressive*, I'd now be charged with maintaining the responsibilities of the quarterly visit to corporate that normally routed to my boss. It was a responsibility that she was eager to unload, the stresses of travel and reporting being something that she had never quite felt comfortable enough in engaging.

"But Jane...you just have this natural power of... hell I don't even know what to call it, girl. But you've got it. The X factor and as such..." Robyn prattled along, any words said after such I tuned out in favor of screaming internally in frustration.

The clearing of her throat indicated that Robyn was done speaking and she looked at me expectantly.

"Is saying no an option?" I asked.

"It absolutely is not," Robyn giggled, "But, you should look at it as an opportunity for a free trip every three months for you to get away and relax a bit."

"Robbie, you know I have responsibilities that kind of...preclude my ability to do that."

"I get it, Jane. I really do. But I also know that you have folks in your corner that will pick up the slack when you're unable to."

I rolled my eyes, grumbling about the perils of working with family. Robyn was not only my boss, but my sister-in-law as well.

"Stop trying to be the big little boss and please do me this solid, J. I mean, honestly, the last time you went up there you came back glowing, so the trip couldn't have been all bad."

Immediately my face grew hot as I recalled the last trip I'd made to corporate. And the ending to that trip that I couldn't have even imagined. Nigel's smooth, dark skin immediately flashed in my mind before I shook my head. That man probably banged lonely, thirsty hotel guests on the regular and I was foolish to even be thinking about him beyond that night. He'd shown me a good time though, Robyn definitely had that part right.

"I mean...besides being impossibly bored in days full of meetings I did manage to have a little fun," I said.

"Okay, so have a little more. Besides, I thought you said you could never get tired of visiting New York because there's so much to do there. Prove it," Robyn teased.

"Ugh, fine, whatever," I said, rising and turning to head out.

"Your flight leaves next Sunday night. Pam will email you with the details."

"Wait, Sunday?"

"Yeah, since this quarter falls at the same time as

the fiscal year ends, the gathering is actually a week-long one instead of the normal couple of days."

You've got to me kidding me I thought with an eyeroll as I left Robyn's office. Not only had I gotten roped into doing some shit I didn't want to do but I never had a choice in the matter anyway since she'd made an executive decision for me. I needed to reach out to Eb and let her know that I'd be back in the City and since her kids were with their daddy's people for the whole damned summer, she should be able to get away and come get into some shenanigans with me. Instead of heading back to my desk, I diverted into one of the library salon rooms that were supplied for us to take and make personal phone calls.

"Ebby!" I screeched once she'd answered in lieu of greeting.

"You're...in a chipper mood. This is new. Blink twice if everything is okay with you," Ebonée ordered, a slight bit of concern coloring her tone.

"You are really annoying. I'm not that bad...am I?"

"You have been, love. But whatever has caused this sudden change in you, I love to see it. So, what's up?"

"What are you doing two weekends from now?" I asked.

"Hopefully getting rooted in a hut in Bali," Eb replied, giggling.

"Oh hell. I forgot your lil man was whisking you off for a romantical getaway."

"Wow, my lil man? Really, J?"

"I'm being a hater. Don't mind me. I'm being sent back to corporate. Apparently I made such an impression last time that I'm now our branch's liaison for the quarterly check-in instead of Robbie, so...I'll be in the City and was going to see if we could get a re-do of our previously rescheduled negro Thelma and Louise shenanigans, but I...guess not."

"I really do not understand why they really fly

someone out from each region quarterly like Skype doesn't exist, but not my monkey, not my show. Sorry, babe. I wish I was gonna be in town, we really are overdue a girls' trip."

"Honestly..."

"But..." Ebonée started with mischief in her voice that I knew meant nothing but trouble.

"But?" I prodded.

"Might be able to bounce that ass on bouncer bae again," she chuckled.

I rolled my eyes, "I swear I cannot stand you."

"We both know that's a lie and that it's also something that ran through your mind at least once since you've heard about this trip."

"I can neither confirm nor deny the veracity of your statement."

"Ooh, she's giving me corporate barbie. I must've really struck a nerve. I mean, I'm just saying for someone who alleges that a random stranger gave her the best dick of her life. If it were me? I'd be rushing back to ride that thang like a motorbike."

"I..." I started but honestly had nothing further to add to this conversation.

"You?" Eb prompted.

"Anyway, well I guess I will have to look into what I can get into when I'm in town. Check out a Broadway show or something."

"You staying at the same place as last time?'

I shrugged like she could see me, "I'm not sure actually. I haven't gotten any of the details of my itinerary."

"I mean, it's most likely since the company is making all of the accommodations that you'll be at the same place as last time. They probably have some sort of relationship with that hotel. Didn't you say it was super close to you guys' corporate office out there too?"

"Yep, just a few blocks away."

"And *he* worked there?" Ebonée asked.

"I'm not entertaining this. I...I gotta go, Eb."

"You're lying because you don't want to have this discussion, but that's okay. If I don't talk to you again before your trip—have fun, be safe, and at least make the effort to get back on that baloney pony, friend. I don't think I've ever heard you sound more...laidback than when you recounted your hotivities to me. Embrace your inner hoe for the culture...or something."

"Bye Eb, love you."

"Love you too, friend. Please take my advice," Ebonee responded before hanging up in my face.

* * *

Whoever said summertime in New York City was the place to be was a freaking liar. In the four days that I'd been in this town I was fucking over it. No wonder natives got up in arms about transplants coming here and complaining. They had to deal with them and the onslaught of tourists that made it nearly impossible to actually enjoy oneself in the more populated areas of the city. I called myself being cultured and taking in shows every night after work since our job had a TKTS hookup that got me great seats for low, low prices, but after being wedged between Norm and Nancy from Nebraska at the last show I attended I was over it all and ready to go home. Friday was set to be an abbreviated workday since I was also traveling back home that day, so I decided to indulge in a little nightcap situation before tucking in for the night.

The rooftop bar was decidedly less clubby on a Thursday evening, with just a handful of folks populating the space, so there was no need for a doorman or bouncer dude. I'd purposefully been avoiding eating or drinking at places in the hotel in the off chance that I might run into Nigel again. It was stupid, honestly, to think that I was that memorable that folks would readily recall me from three months ago. As I slid onto the barstool and signaled to the bartender however, that little hypothesis was blown to smithereens.

"PJ! You're back," Abril crooned, wiping the bar top in front of me and setting down a coaster, "You want your usual?"

"Ok, first of all...I'd have to be a regular to have a 'usual' and I hardly think that three visits to a place would make me a regular," I laughed, "And no, I will not be having that damned Truth Serum. I got into trouble off of those last time. Let me just get a G&T."

Abril arched a brow, "I'll have you know; the truth serum doesn't do anything that the drinker of said serum doesn't want to do. And everyone knows...it's gin that'll make you sin while you're ordering a gin and tonic. Let me make you a special drink. Not the Truth Serum, but equally delicious."

She stood there with a toothy grin splitting her face open that made it damn near impossible for me to say no to her request. I nodded my head in acquiescence and took a brief gander around the bar while Abril made my drink. By the time she made it back with my drink, I felt less like sitting up here and drinking it and more like taking my ass back down to my room. I wasn't fooling myself, the only reason I'd ventured up here was on the off chance that I'd see *him* again. The moment it became clear that I wasn't going to, I'd lost all my gumption.

"Y'all don't do to go cups for guests of the hotel do you, Spanish April?" I asked, with a chuckle.

She shook her head, laughing, "Nah, doll. I can't let you leave here with anything you didn't come with...unless it's a man. I can't stop that from happening."

I joined her giggles halfheartedly.

"Damn, tough crowd," Abril quipped.

I shook my head, "Nah, that was actually pretty good. I'm just...feeling a way right now is all. I'm ready to go home, actually. I've been in town all week and this pace of New York City? I can't keep up. I gotta get back to my slow rolling, suburbanite existence."

"Where are you from originally?"

"The Midwest, just outside of Chicago, actually. From a suburb that white folks from Chicago try to claim *is* Chicago when they're out of town and telling folks where they're from."

"That managed to be very specific, but broad as hell. You sound like a spin doctor, what do you do for a living?"

"Damn, is this the Spanish Inquisition?" I joked.

Abril gestured around, "It's slow as hell in here, mama. It's either keep bothering you or make Nigel come from in back playing Candy Crush and fake bounce at the door."

At the mention of his name, I perked up a bit.

"Nigel?" I asked, trying to sound casual.

"Mmmhmmm, the fine ass bouncer. You remember him. I *know* you do," Abril sassed.

"What's that supposed to mean?" I asked, slightly shook.

I didn't think I was that transparent and I'd only been in here a few minutes. Did I give off desperate, stalker bitch vibes?

"Girl, please. You'd have to have the memory of Dory from Finding Nemo to forget how Nigel's ass looks."

"Are you two..." I asked, trailing off, not even exactly sure what the hell I was getting ready to ask.

Whatever and however those two got along was no business of mine. Nothing to do with Nigel beyond that one night we shared was any business of mine.

Abril shook her head, grimacing, "Nah...he's got a real dick; not a plasdick. I can't."

I nearly spit out the sip of the very delicious cocktail that Abril had brought me.

"Did you just say plasdick?"

She nodded, "I hate whenever Shane refers to her strap as her plasdick, but I'll be damned if sometimes there's no other word to use."

I was doubled over laughing, damn near losing my breath at her ridiculousness. Once I gathered my composure, I begged her to stop. I didn't know how much more of this I could l take nor how far Abril would take talking about this plasdick she spoke of. Abril went back and forth between me and the only other patrons in the spot, a couple sitting on the opposite end of the bar from me. I only stayed up there long enough to finish my drink and pop out to the upper rooftop to get a flick of the immaculate view of Manhattan that was only visible from that space. As I turned to pick my way back the narrow staircase that would take me to the bar level elevator, I heard a voice ask, "You're leaving already?"

Before I could fully turn around, he was all in my space, crowding me. I stepped back slightly, craning my head up to look him in the eye as I rested against the bricks of the building's roof ledge.

"Nigel, right?" I asked, knowing damn well who he was.

He chuckled, "Damn, was I that forgettable?"

Actually, quite the opposite sir I thought but instead spoke, "I'm terrible with names."

"Abril told me you came back. I thought she was lying," Nigel said, closing that intentional space I'd put between us, "How you been, miss lady?"

My nose wrinkled, "Miss Lady?"

Nigel chuckled, a low rumbling sound that raced straight through me.

"I didn't forget your name, Jane. If that's what

you're thinking," he said, reaching out to run his hand down my arm, grabbing my hand and lacing our fingers together, "And if the energy between us I'm feeling is any indication, you didn't forget my name either. Your little amnesia act is cute though."

"I..." I opened my mouth to start a lie, but before I could complete it, Nigel lowered his mouth to mine, kissing whatever excuse was about to come out away. My body didn't get my mind's memo to play it cool as I plastered myself against his large frame, getting as close as I possibly could. Nigel's large, nimble hands traversed my body slowly as our tongues tangled before settling his grip upon my ass. We continued on making out like teenagers until I finally pulled back to catch my breath. Chest heaving, I struggled to get my breathing under control for a minute or two.

"On second thought...that apology from before wasn't good enough," Nigel said suddenly, "Can I get a do over?"

I dropped my head, giggling before looking back up at him through lowered lids with my bottom lip cinched between my teeth. I didn't trust my voice not to tremble or squeak, so I just offered him a nod in response. I reached into my clutch, sliding the extra key I'd prophetically asked for at check in out of the sleeve in which it'd been housed all week and passing it Nigel's way.

"Room number?" he asked.

"Eight eighteen."

"Bet. I'll be there as soon as I'm done for the night," Nigel said before escorting me back down into the main bar and onto the elevator.

It didn't hit me until I had been back in my room for about twenty minutes that I never settled up with Abril for my drink. Freshly showered, I threw on a simple wrap dress and some flip flop sandals to run back up there and handle that, but as I was about to leave, the sensor on the door was triggered and Nigel was stepping into my room.

"Where you are goin'? You were about to sneak out on me again?" he asked, grinning as he ran a hand down the back of his head.

I couldn't help but return his grin as I answered, "No, I was going to settle up with Abril since somebody hustled me out of the bar before I could cover my tab."

Nigel continued to back me into the room, kicking the door shut behind him and turning to engage the deadbolt.

"Nah, you're good, sweetheart. Trust me," he said.

And for some strange ass reason, I did. So, I let him lead me backward onto the bed where he easily covered my body with his as he joined our mouths together once again. Something about this kiss seemed less urgent than the one of the rooftop, as if he was taking his time committing every crevice of my mouth to memory as his tongue licked, sucked, and darted around my mouth's depths in search of some long buried treasure. His hands fisted in my hair, angling my neck upward as he moved his trailing tongue from my mouth down to my neck, plying it with open mouthed suckles that were sure to leave a mark, but I couldn't be bothered to give a damn because what he was doing felt so damn good. Praise and adulations fell from my lips as I begged him to never stop doing what he was doing.

And stopping was the furthest thing from his mind if the vigor with which he removed my clothing was any indication. The growl that came from him when he realized I was completely nude beneath my dress sent a shiver through me.

"You been outside all day like this?" he groaned, palming my breasts in each of his hands.

"N-no, I just," the words of explanation I was going to offer dying on my lips when his tongue made contact with my breast, circling the areola with the tip then curling his tongue around my nipple to give a hard suckle. He repeated that movement on the other side and I arched upward toward his mouth, not wanting the sensations his mouth evoked to dissipate. My hands flew to the back of his head to keep him in place and a sly chuckle escaped before Nigel commenced to feasting on my body like it was a gourmet meal. No piece of my skin was left untouched by his hands, mouth, or some mindblowing amazing combination of the two. By the time he reached my center, I was panting with anticipation, my memory of his time spent dining at my y during our last encounter at the forefront of my mind. As if he could read my mind, Nigel peered up at me as he spread my legs wide, a devious smirk on his lips. A breath I hadn't realized I was holding was slowly expelled as he settled an elbow upon each of my knees and lowered his face to my pussy. Instead of diving in face first as he had the last time, he hovered briefly, a groan of anticipation escaping me as I felt his inhalations and exhalations teasing my lower lips.

"Nigel, please," I whined, not caring how desperate I sounded.

I tried arching up toward his mouth, ruining his delay of my inevitable pleasure, but I underestimated his power play of bracing his forearms on my inner thighs as he settled between my legs.

"Can't rush my appreciation of fine art, sweetheart," Nigel crooned.

"And this," he said, using two fingers to spread my pussy apart, "is one of the finest pieces of work I've seen in quite some time."

I had no rebuttal as he'd barely gotten the last word out of his mouth before he lowered his face and placed an open-mouthed kiss directly on my clit. The dual sensations of the rasp of his tongue against my button and his soft, downy facial hair tickling me had me damn near ready to sign over my 401k to this nigga just to have access to this tongue on demand. And when he added his fingers to the party, I was sad that I hadn't yet added him as beneficiary to my life insurance plan because he was definitely trying to kill me, but what a damn way to go. I wasn't the only one enjoying myself as Nigel moaned in delight, expresseing just how sweet my pussy was to him. I felt myself on the precipice of cumming when he did something with his tongue that had me seeing stars while my thighs convulsed like I was having a seizure. I couldn't even formulate words, just an endless stream of screaming jibberish as I shuddered my way through an orgasm.

Minutes later, I opened my eyes to see Nigel standing in front of the bed, fully nude, just staring down upon my naked form as he rubbed his chin.

"Welcome back," he chuckled.

I sat up, groaning in embarrassment at his teasing before crooking a finger in his direction for him to rejoin me on the bed. As soon as he was within arm's reach, a burst of energy shot through me and I attacked him, hellbent on making him feel half as good as he'd made me feel. Straddling his lap, I kissed my way down his body until I reached his dick. Wrapping one hand around it...or at least attempting to as my fingers barely touched...I pumped once, slowly. Nigel placed a hand over mine, adjusting the pressure I applied to his liking. The softly muttered curses that left his mouth as my hand caught a rhythm turned into a harsh groan as I took him in my mouth, attempting to swallow him whole. He had entirely too much dick for me to be able to so effectively, but I definitely had fun trying to meet the challenge.

"Shit, sweetheart," Nigel groaned as I released his dick from my mouth with a pop before going right back to work.

With a hand tangled in my curls, Nigel held me in

place as he pumped his hips upward in slow, rolling strokes. I shook his hands off, looking up at him with a scowl before getting back to the task at hand. Using my hands and mouth, I stoked him to the brink of insanity until he was warning me that he was about to cum. Sane me would have politely moved out of the way and let his nut land where it may, but this brazen, dick starved me kept my mouth right the fuck where it was, swallowing down every bit of cum that spurted forth, licking my lips in satisfaction when the eruption ceased. There was a little bit still seeping from him when I removed my mouth completely, so I darted my tongue out to lap it up. The movement elicited a rough, throaty chuckle from Nigel as I moved to line my face back up with his and leaned in for a kiss. He took my mouth greedily, guiding me to straddle him. Once again, he plied my mouth with those slow, suckling kisses. Unhurried swipes of his tongue in my mouth like we had all night and the rest of our lives to remain like this, wrapped in each other's arms.

I was more interested in getting to the main event, as his dick came back life beneath my ass cheeks while I writhed in his lap. I pulled back from his kisses long enough to inquire about a condom and he gestured toward the nightstand alongside the bed. I made quick work of reaching over, sheathing him and sliding down onto him until I was fully seated. We shared twin grins and groans of contentment as our bodies became reacquainted with one another. I rocked against him with the slightest hitch of my hips as my body adjusted to his size. Soon, that slight rocking gave way to full on hip rolls that Nigel met with upward thrusts of his own before he flipped us completely over and took control. He wrapped my legs around his waist and I easily acquiesced, succumbing to the pleasure he doled out with each thrust into my body.

"You kept this pussy tight for me, huh, baby?" Nigel gritted out, slow stroking me into complete ecstasy.

I opened my mouth to answer him, but all that came out was a loud hum as he shifted my legs from his waist to rest in the crook of his arms as he plummeted even further into my depths. The change in angle felt like he was trying to drill his way into the center of my body using his dick. He persisted with his line of questioning, demanding an answer, but I was rendered completely incoherent with each thrust of his hips. I came on a strangled moan, body arching up from the bed as I released. Nigel kept stroking, setting off a second combustion when he finally drove into me with one final thrust, growling through his own completion. Immediately thereafter, he collapsed onto me, his weighty frame a welcomed intrusion as we both came back to ourselves. A few moments passed before Nigel withdrew from me and urged me out of the bed and into the bathroom. On jellied legs I allowed him to lead me into the shower, where we spent more time groping one another before finally cleansing our bodies and falling into bed again.

I awakened the next morning before my alarm went off to an empty bed. Last night felt entirely too real for it to have been an elaborate dream sequence. I sat up with a yawn, rolling my neck before swinging my legs out of bed so I could get up to start my day. I was tired as hell, but after being piped down for the majority of the night, I couldn't help the grin that was plastered to my face.

"Somebody's in a good mood," Nigel's low voice rumbled.

I jumped in shock. I'd assumed that the empty bed meant he'd left under the cover of night or, rather during dawn's earliest light since we'd barely dozed off at about three in the morning.

"Sheesh!" I giggled, still clutching at the invisible pearls around my neck, "you just scared the shit outta me."

Nigel chuckled, moving across the room to pull me into an embrace.

"Damn, what kinda grimy dude do you think I am that I'd just take off like a thief in the night without letting you know?"

"I..."

"Uh huh, don't try to clean it up now," he said, leaning down to press a soft kiss on my partially opened lips, "Good morning, by the way. Hope you don't mind me crashing since somebody wore me out last night."

I dropped my head, a smirk of amusement gracing my lips when I finally raised my head again.

"I heard no complaints last night," I giggled.

"Won't hear any this morning either..." Nigel shot back as his hands moved from their perch at my waist down to my ass.

"As...tempting as that offer is, we can't. I've got to be at the office in," I said, peering over his shoulder to view the analog clock on the nightstand, "an hour and fifteen minutes. And since somebody tangled my hair into a matted mess...I need all of that time to get my life together and get ready."

"What time are you off? I'm off today and I'd like to see you again. Wait...that sounds thirstier than I actually planned for it to sound but fuck it. It's the truth. So whassup?"

I grimaced knowing that I was on my way home after working 'til eleven at the office today. I communicated that much to Nigel and he brushed me off.

"Just change your flight," he insisted, "Stay the weekend. With me."

"Um...it's not quite that easy. I didn't make the reservations; everything was handled through my boss' assistant. And, I know you know from working here that this place isn't exactly cheap to stay in, let alone on a weekend."

"Who said anything about staying here? I said *stay with me*," Nigel reasoned, "Look, I'm just gonna keep straight up with you, Jane. There's...something here. I know you feel it. I know it isn't just one-sided."

And he was one hundred percent on point with that. We hadn't spent the entire night just sexing each other out of our minds. We'd also done a lot of chatting, at first about mindless subjects that meant little to nothing, but eventually diverting into heavier and deeper subjects like the current state of this nation, our political ideologies, future goals and things like that. It was strange to get that deep with a virtual stranger, but I also figured since I'd taken his uncovered penis into my mouth without reservation, there wasn't much that I couldn't share with this man. It was weird how comfortable I felt with him almost immediately. I told myself that I was reading too much into it, that he was just an incredibly cool man who made it easy to talk to him. But when Nigel put into words the exact thoughts that had been running through my mind?

"So, let me get this straight. You expect me to spend money to change my flight home or purchase a one-way ticket and then come lay up in a stranger's apartment in a city that is thousands of miles away from my home? How do I know you're not some serial killer who woos unsuspecting women with amazing sex?"

Nigel erupted with a roar of laughter, shaking his head, "You wild, sweetheart. I never said anything about any of this being your expense. I'm asking you to stay and trust that I'll take care of the rest."

"I watch Dateline and 20/20. I know how this goes. I'm woke."

Nigel continued laughing, "So woke that you invited a man whose last name you don't even know back to your hotel room *twice* to blow ya back out."

"You know you're not helping your case with that little statement, right?" I giggled.

"Just laying out the facts here, ma'am. If I was gonna serial murder you, I was already given two occasions on which I could do it. But enough of this back and forth. Look we can call my mama right now if you need someone to vouch for me. I'll let you send scans of my driver's license to ya peoples. Whatever I need to do to get you to stay, I'll do it, Jane. I'm so serious."

"I...you're laying it on mighty thick, sir," I stalled, trying not to let the giddiness I felt at his strong declarations show too much on my face.

"But it's working isn't it?"

"We'll see..."

Those two words turned into me calling Nigel at the time I was supposed to be on my way to JFK Airport and letting him know that I'd left the office and would soon be on the way to his place.

Q3: OCTOBER

"I'm...not...oh my God, how did we even get here?" I asked, covering my face as I turned away from Nigel.

"Nah...where's Brazen Jane that handed me her keycard six months ago, bring her back because you pump faking. Talked all that shit before you got here and yet here you are, in my presence, and *all of a sudden...*"

I turned back toward him and mugged, "You know when you asked me to come out here early so we could have some quality time, I can't say that this was anything I could have ever anticipated happening."

Unfazed, he reached over and pulled me closer to him on the couch, pressing a sweet, fleeting kiss to my forehead that belied the downright filthy situation in which we found ourselves currently. Another quarter had passed, and Nigel and I were...kinda sorta dating ish? As much as two people who lived just under a thousand miles away from one another could date, anyway. We spent entirely too much time caking with one another daily—either through text or FaceTime. I felt like I was right back in junior high school with my first crush. I was equal parts fascinated and hopeful, yet anxious and fearful still. This fine, smart-mouthed, multi-dimensionally talented and intelligent man was giving me so much—time, energy, effort that it was kind of overwhelming. I was constantly waiting for the other shoe to drop. He'd yet to make the trek out my way, but for this quarterly visit I decided to use up a couple of days of paid time off and extend our time together. Which was how I found myself in a state of barely dressed, lounging in the midst of what looked like a damned spaceship with all of the technology he had laying around in various states in here.

The bouncer gig? A side job that was a favor to a friend whose family owned the hotel in which I found myself staying every time my job sent me to the city. Nigel actually owned his own company, which specialized in building custom computer systems for serious gamers. Over the past few months I'd heard more about gigabytes and whatever the hell else he dealt in and desperately tried keeping up. No matter how many times he tried to dumb it down for me, I just couldn't seem to grasp hold of anything he was talking about. But the passion with which he spoke when he got to talking about his work was damn near as engaging as the passion he exuded in the bedroom, so I was rapt every time we went down this rabbit hole, even if I had zero idea what was going on. Now, however, we were talking about something far removed from technology related to his work.

"You're stalling, love," Nigel crooned, capturing my earlobe between his teeth and biting down gently.

I shivered in response to the contact before responding, "You first."

"Aight, bet," he replied confidently, "Gimme the iPad".

He had a dope little set up in his crib with a projector system instead of a regular television screen. On the largest wall of his living room, I watched as he opened up Safari and navigated to some site called tastyblacks.com. My eyebrows raised because he was putting me onto some new shit here. I kept it simple, navigating to *SploogeTube* whenever I found myself needing a fix if my mental images didn't do the trick. As the page loaded with category after category featuring beautiful ass brown skin appeared, I wondered how in the hell I'd gone this long without ever knowing this site existed.

"So...depending on my mood I usually start with Big Ass...actually that's a lie. I always start with Big Ass because well...you know...I like big asses."

I turned and buried my head into his chest as he went on and on about his preferred porn categories, the type of lotion he used to jack himself off, how he switches up with the intensity and speed of the strokes of his hand. This negro really sat here breaking it down, pontificating on the evolution of porn and the advantages of the rise of amateur content. I wanted to be stunned, but he'd made such... salient points that I found myself becoming less uptight about discussing and sharing my preferences with him.

"So...no judgement, yeah?"

"Baby, I just told you about my creampie obsession. Who am I to judge anything you got to share... unless you into some real depraved shit like scat. Wait...you ain't into..." he trailed off.

"Ugh, God, no Nigel," I shrieked, slapping him across the chest, "why would you think?"

"Hey...this is still pretty new, sweetheart. Who knows what skeletons you're hiding in ya freak chifforobe!"

"Did you just say chifforobe?"

"Stay focused, JBaby. What are your categories?"

I motioned for him to hand over the iPad, "Well. First of all, I'm super mad that I've been suffering through so much pink penis only to discover that there's a whole treasure trove of black on black goodness that I don't have to filter to the high heavens to find something to get me off. Wow. A whole new world opened right before my eyes."

"Well actually, it an aggregator so a lot of the videos you know and love are probably over on TB as well."

"Ok, so I really don't have categories as much as like...pointed search terms. I've...amassed a few favorites that I fall back on."

"You're procrastinating with all this talking baby, just pull up a flick," Nigel muttered into my neck before pressing a series of lingering kisses there.

"Or we could just go make one ourselves," I said, angling my neck so that he had better access.

He stopped suddenly pulling back and looking at me, "Word?"

I bit my lower lip, nodding. It was something I'd been thinking about for a while actually. Nigel had a way of making me feel like I was the hottest bitch in the world whenever he laid hands on me. Because I knew how good I felt when we were being intimate, I wanted to see if it looked as good as it felt, too.

"Brazen Jane is back in the building, ladies and gentlemen!" Nigel crowed.

"Oh my god, shut up before I change my mind."

"Too late, sweetheart," he said, snatching me up from the couch and throwing me over his shoulder. I dropped the iPad onto the couch so I could hold onto him and he moved us through his apartment to his bedroom located in a lofted area of his apartment. His place was gorgeous, airy and spacious in an old building converted from a factory to lofts—tons of exposed brick and metal accents all over the place as the integrity of the original structure was left almost completely unmolested upon conversion. When we made it to his bed and he laid me out, I looked over to see his camera already poised on a tripod on his dresser.

"You...uh...clairvoyant or something?" I giggled, nodding toward the camera.

Nigel chuckled, "You know what they say...stay ready so you ain't gotta get ready."

"Seriously?" I asked, sitting up from my previously reclined position.

Nigel leaned down and placed a soft kiss on my lips, "No, crazy girl. I was recording some footage of this system I'm building over there for my YouTube channel."

"Mmmmhmmm, whatever you say. I've got my eye on you," I laughed.

"Got your eye on me but you the one over here with your *press record I'll let you film me on your video phone* energy..."

"Did you just quote a Beyoncé song?"

"Stop trying to derail and get naked, girl."

I laughed, shaking my head, "You want me naked, you gotta take these clothes off of me."

Clothes was an overstatement, as I was clad in what had become sort of my uniform while at Nigel's place. One of his tee shirts with nothing underneath and a pair of his socks pulled damn near up to my thighs because he kept this place freezing cold.

"That ain't no problem at all," Nigel said, a sly smirk curving his mouth, "Lemme just..."

He moved the camera from its perch on his dresser to the other side of the room onto his desk where it would have a panoramic view of his bed. He adjusted a few settings, all the while teasing me about how he was gonna tear my ass up, so it looked good on the playback. I playfully flirted back, trying to fight through the nerves that appeared now that this wasn't just an abstract idea but was actually happening. When he finally had the camera situated to his liking, he dropped the ball shorts he was wearing and strolled over to the bed beautifully nude. Nigel was a big dude, built like a former defensive end, tall and super thick but not overly muscular. And as the scant sunlight streamed through his blinds, illuminating his body as he strode over to me, I sent a quick prayer of thanks for this physical manifestation of a dream I didn't even know I'd wanted coming true. Those previous nerves dissipated as soon as he was in arm's reach. I crawled to the end of the bed to meet him and before he could place a limb on the bed to join me, my mouth was on him—taking his dick as far down my throat as it could go.

"Goddamn, Jane," Nigel moaned.

I pulled back slowly, lightly grazing his shaft with my teeth as I withdrew him from my mouth. Looking directly into his eyes, I swirled the tip of my tongue around the head of his dick slowly before deep throating him again and going to work. He soon caught the rhythm of my bobs, thrusting his hips forward in time with the movement of my mouth. My hands were braced around his thighs and I could feel the muscles tightening, signaling he was close to release when he suddenly yanked me off of his dick by my hair, grumbling something about not going out like a sucker on film. In what seemed like a nanosecond, he'd stripped me completely bare and buried his face between my legs, his tongue moving like he was seeking buried treasure in my pussy. I tried moving out of his grasp, the prolonged flickering of his tongue against my pearl sparking too much pleasure for me to bear, but that only caused him to go harder.

"Don't run from it," he crooned, removing his mouth from my pussy and replacing it with his fingers, "You asked for this, didn't you?"

He didn't give me a chance to answer, pressing his mouth to mine, swallowing any words of rebuttal I would have tried to form. His fingers worked me back up to fever pitch, moving in and out of my slit at a maddeningly slow pace as his thumb circled my clit in barely there swipes.

"Ssssss," I hissed when he finally disconnected our mouths, to catch a breath.

"What's that, babe?" he asked, increasing the speed of his pistoning fingers.

My mouth hung open, but no sound emitted as I gasped at the sensation of his fingers inside of my core, driving me out of my mind. He added a third finger and stroked slightly deeper, which was all I needed to completely send me over the edge. I came with a sharp cry, arching from the bed like I'd been jolted by electricity. My reaching the summit didn't faze Nigel one bit as he kept on stroking me with his fingers, setting off aftershocks before urging me up on onto my knees. A firm hand on my upper back guided me to lower myself to my elbows, while keeping my ass lifted up in the air.

"Don't move," Nigel growled, the gruffness in his tone inciting another round of shivers to pass through my body.

After a few moments of no movement from Nigel, I chanced a look back and was met with a firm smack to my ass. The dual sensations of pleasure and pain drew a low groan from me as I thrust my ass backward even further hoping this movement brought forth another of those deliciously painful smacks. Nigel chuckled instead.

"Oh, that's your shit, huh? Noted," he said, urging me back into the position he'd initially put me in and quickly sliding his dick deep inside of me.

He dicked me down ferociously, unrepentantly driving into me with breath robbing strokes at a breakneck speed. Each thrust sent his balls flying upward, slapping against my clit, adding to the already overwhelming onslaught of pleasure I was experiencing. Soon my arms gave out, but that didn't deter Nigel as his grip on my hips tightened and he slowed the measure of his strokes. Something about this coupling felt different, more intense...more...intimate.

Nigel switched our positions once again, without withdrawing from deep within me. As he guided me to lay on my left side, then hooked an arm under my right thigh, I looked down greedily enjoying the view of his dick sliding in and out of the mess of wetness between my thighs. It was at this point that I realized why it felt so different was because he hadn't put on a condom, but I was too far gone to even give a damn at this point. The change in position gave me a bit of leverage as I contracted around him with each stroke, making his withdrawal from my body more arduous each time he dove back in. Those contractions soon drove him to the brink, and he whispered in my ear on a guttural groan that he was about to cum and I whispered back to him words I hadn't ever uttered to a man.

"I want to feel you come inside of me," I moaned, tightening my pelvic muscles once again.

The combination of those words and that action were the magic words that unlocked his orgasm. With one last powerful thrust into my core, Nigel came inside of me with a ragged groan, setting off yet another orgasm for me. As I quivered my way through release, Nigel released the hold he had on my leg, but stayed inside of me. Pressing a kiss to my shoulder blade that sent a shiver through me, Nigel whispered in my ear, "I cannot wait to watch this back, babe. We might win an AVN for this shit."

I couldn't help but giggle at his silly ass, "Something is wrong with you."

"Or," he started, pressing another of those gentle kisses to my shoulder before sliding out of me, "is everything right, baby?"

I watched him walk over to stop the camera and couldn't help but chuckle to myself at his mostly hard dick still jutting forth from his body like he was ready for more action. He disappeared into the bathroom and I heard the shower start before he came back out to me. Slapping me on the ass he ordered me up and into the shower while he stripped the sheets from the bed. I dragged myself into his beautifully tiled shower and found the grin that had been on my face since we'd finished growing broader when I noticed that he'd had the specialty body wash and shampoo that I mentioned to him that I use on the built-in shelving in the shower, along with Salux cloths.

"Okay, Mr. Cook, score one for you," I murmured under my breath as the door to the stall opened and Nigel stepped in.

"Figured we could...conserve some water, you know? That is...if you can keep your hands to yourself, ma'am. No funny business, I'm just here to get clean—dassit."

I just shook my head, moving aside so he could come in completely and shut the door.

* * *

I never made it to the room that work reserved for me. Since the hotel had found a new, full-time bouncer Nigel had a lot more time on his hands. And with that time, he convinced me to stay at his place while I was in town for work, providing me with a ride to and from the office for the two days that I'd had to attend meetings. It was...awfully cozy and honestly felt too good for me to want to leave behind when I had to travel back home. So, I tried to keep that out of my mind, instead choosing to relish this time that we were spending together and knowing that we were working toward something. What that something was? I wasn't exactly sure yet, but I was hopeful. More hopeful than I'd been in a while with anything regarding a man. I was still hesitant to put a label on what was happening here, though. I was cautiously optimistic.

I was currently lounging on Nigel's couch waiting

for him to return with some dinner. He insisted on going out to grab some Jamaican food from a spot he swore was the bomb, but the two other times this week we'd tried to eat there? They were out of damn near all of their main dishes. He was bound and determined to prove to me that their food was slap your mama good though, so I acquiesced. I knew one thing for sure though. If he didn't come back in here with some damn oxtails and rice and peas tonight? I was gonna be pissed. After he'd been hyping it up all day, it was all my mouth was set for now. Until he returned, I was fully entrenched in a marathon of *Let Me Upgrade You with Will & Way*. I had the biggest crush on these identical twin negro property brothers, and I had to get my viewing of them out of my system before Nigel returned. He wasn't too fond of my slight obsession.

As I sat watching Will & Way, my FaceTime tone sounded off. I fully expected it to be Nigel calling to tell me that the Jamaican spot was coming up short again but was pleasantly surprised to see it was Ebonée. She and I had been playing phone tag for the past month, so I was definitely catching this call.

"What up, Ebby?" I trilled.

"Oh, you must be fresh off the dick, you're so chipper," Ebonée laughed, "But hello to you too, boo. I don't need to ask how you're doing. That glow on your face is telling me everything I need to know."

"Here you go," I replied, shaking my head.

"Mmmmhmmm, you having fun playing house?"

"Nobody's playing house. I'm visiting a friend," I smiled shyly.

"Girl please, that man being your friend went out the window when you told me that y'all be out here playing the junior high *no you hang up, no you hang up* game out here. Me on the other hand, *your best friend*, has been unable to pin your ass down for a call for weeks but I bet he doesn't have that problem at all, does he? That man ain't just your damn friend. That's your boyfriend, your bae, your booskidoop," Ebonée insisted.

"Booskidoop, Eb?"

"Cute, right? It's got a ring to it," she laughed.

"I just...I don't know what to do with you sometimes," I replied, shaking my head, "But seriously, we haven't put any labels on anything. We're just hanging out, getting to know one another, kicking it as friends. No pressure, no muss no fuss."

"Can I say something? Wait, actually no...I'm not going to ask you for permission. I'm just going to say something to you that I want you to take seriously. Don't slow roll this, friend. I can see a visible change —for the positive—that this man is bringing out in you in multiple ways. Whatever is holding you up or making you feel like you need to downplay this, you need to let that shit go, sis. You deserve this man. You deserve these feelings. You deserve whatever new life is on its way with you accepting the simple fact that Nigel is indeed your man and may very well one day be your husband. And when that day comes that you're walking down the aisle to him, right before the preacher starts up with his lil spiel or whatever, I'm going to lean over to you, grab your bouquet so you and your future husband can hold hands whilst exchanging those vows and whisper, 'I told your ass!' And it'll be glorious."

"Hey baby, the spot wasn't out, and I got your food," Nigel crooned suddenly, and I damn near dropped my phone turning around to see him coming through the door.

I swear the man moved like a ninja because I didn't hear him unlock nor come through the door at all. He made his way over to the couch where I was sitting and dropped a quick kiss on my forehead before proceeding toward the kitchen and dining area to take the foot out of the bags and get us set up for dinner. I wrapped up my call with Eb, with a promise to holler at her again before we got through a new week and walked into the kitchen where Nigel was selecting a bottle of wine. I noticed he hadn't gotten around to setting the table yet, so I grabbed plates and silverware, setting two places for us next to one another on the bench that made up half of his dining area.

"Finally caught up with Eb, huh?" he asked, walking toward the table with the wine and two glasses in his grasp.

"Yep," I said, opening up the to go containers and dishing food onto one of the plates before handing it to Nigel.

He looked over at me in surprise as he uncorked the wine. He poured us each a glass, sliding mine over in my direction before clasping my hands in his to say grace. After we'd prayed over the food, he was still looking at me with a strange little gleam in his eye.

"What?" I asked.

"You made my plate first," he replied.

"Okay, and?"

"Nothing," he said on a chuckle, "Nothing at all, baby."

But it was definitely something. I didn't want to press the issue though. Nigel had no problem expressing himself if he needed to, so I figured that if it was really something, he'd address it head on.

"So, what were you and Ebonée talking about? Any hot gossip from DC?"

I took a sip of wine, shaking my head, "We actually hadn't been on long before you came in, actually."

"Aw, babe, I know you'd been tryna catch up with her for a few weeks, you didn't have to cut it short on my behalf. I wouldn't have been offended if you talked to her for a while longer. We coulda just had dinner in front of the tv."

"Nah...no, we're fine. Eb said more than she needed to say anyway," I muttered.

Nigel said nothing more and neither did I as we sat eating and drinking our wine. He hadn't lied, the Jamaican spot was banging. The oxtail was super tender, damn near melting in my mouth as soon as it hit my tongue. Rice and peas were good as hell, too. I let Nigel know as much after I completely destroyed my first plate and low key wanted to go back for seconds, but I was chilling. The next thing I knew, Nigel was dishing more oxtail onto my plate.

"I'm good," I feigned, and he just chuckled.

"You had that look in your eye glancing at that takeout tray, sweetheart. You know the one. It's the same one you hit me with whenever you're ready for...*more of me*. Figured it must translate to food, too."

"You don't want more?" I said, noticing that he'd given me the last bit of oxtail left.

He shook his head, "I'm good love, enjoy."

I smacked my teeth, "Man...come on with that."

"I'm serious though, have at it," Nigel insisted, motioning with his hands for me to get on with it and finish up the food.

He didn't have to tell me anything more as I happily commenced to finishing off the rest of the food and my wine glass that Nigel had refilled. After cleaning up we migrated toward the couch, where Nigel stretched out and I climbed right beside him, snuggling close. I inhaled, trying to be as discreet as possible, but needing to commit the uniquely coded scent of Nigel into the deepest recesses of my memory banks. Who knew when I'd actually be in his presence next and I wanted to be able to hold onto the strongest memories of him.

"Did you just...sniff me?" Nigel laughed.

"I did. But let's not make it weird, okay?" I replied back.

"Sure, you didn't start it off weird or anything."

I groaned, "It's silly. I'm in my head too much. I need to be in the moment, right? Right. Good chat, Nigel."

He tapped me on the ass, nudging me to sit up. He sat up fully too and turned to face me.

"So, you wanna address the elephant in the room or me?" he said.

"Elephant?" I squeaked.

"You don't have a poker face, Jbaby. I could tell something has been in on your mind all week. And I've let you cook, pouting every damn night before we settled down for the night for real. Plus, I kinda heard the tail end of your conversation with Eb."

"How much of that, exactly?" I asked, pulling back slightly.

Nigel shook his head, grasping my hands tighter, erasing my attempt to put some distance between us.

"I heard you playin' me off," Nigel said coolly, pitching his voice a little higher, "We're just kicking it. No muss no fuss."

"I..."

"Mmmmmhmmmm, yeah you were playing me off like you don't know what it is. But that's cool because that's your M.O.," he placed a hand under my chin and moved in closer to whisper, "Be clear, sweetheart. You're mine."

"And what does being *yours* mean, exactly?" I whispered, needing clarity, hell surety that I wasn't being presumptuous.

"It means," he said, pressing his lips against mine once...then once more, "that I'm courting you...long distance until one or the other of us gets over being a punk and decides to push us to take this to the next level. I'm tryna be ya booskidoop out here, girl."

"Oh, your ass heard more than about half," I smirked.

"So whassup? You tryna make me yours too or nah? I'm out here choosing alone?"

I bit my lower lip shaking my head.

"Nah, sweetheart. I'ma need you to use your words," Nigel prodded, "So whassup?"

I grinned, kissing him softly before pulling back to whisper, "Well I did let you raw dog me on camera. So, I guess you're mine, too!"

Nigel immediately erupted with a shout of laughter once my words registered, doubling over from how hard he was laughing. I couldn't help but join him in the laughter, especially when he completely lost the ability to tamp down his laughter and tears streamed from his eyes. After a few moments more of hysteria, we both finally managed to pull ourselves together and sat grinning at each other looking foolish.

"So, we're good here? We're clear?" Nigel asked.

"Yes, Nigel, we are super clear," I droned.

"Wait...I got two more things we need to settle," Nigel said, suddenly.

"Okay," I replied, feeling the crease between my brows deepen before I could control it.

"One," he started holding up one of those long ass index fingers of his, "This Nigel shit has got to go. I always feel like I'm being reprimanded. What you got against nicknames? Dang! Always so formal."

I snickered, shaking my head at his silly ass, "You got suggestions?"

"Anything but daddy. That shit is creepy to me, straight up."

I pitched my voice higher and drawled, "Really, zaddy?"

The immediate lust that flared in Nigel's eyes betrayed his earlier words.

"Well, you know a man can be wrong every now and again," he joked.

"I'm not gonna call you daddy seriously. I think

that's wild creepy as well. I gotta think on this, though. What was your second thing?"

"Oh," he smirked, "I was gonna say that since me 'raw dogging you on film' was the way you made it official, that we should finally relive the moment. Gone ahead and finally watch our art..."

"Or," I replied, reaching up to bring his face closer to mine, "we can make another one."

"Say less, sweetheart," Nigel replied, snatching me up from the couch and throwing me over one of his shoulders, "You ain't said nothin' but a word!"

That night...was the beginning of the shift between me and Nigel. My flight to get back home seemed like it was the most arduous task ever since I hadn't wanted to leave his side. But home was where my life was permanently situated, despite Nigel rapidly becoming a very integral part of my world. Each time I traveled back home from the City I was torn between feeling bereft and guilty. The unfettered joy I felt in Nigel's presence sparked immense guilt because he seemed like a heaven-sent miracle and I'd already been the recipient of a pretty major one of those about eighteen months ago. Ever since then I felt like I was pressing my luck, feeling like the backswing of nearly escaping death definitely would have a tremendous effect in my life going forward.

I was in the car with my dad, on our way out to dinner to accept the position I'd accepted as account executive at my sister in law's family's marketing firm. It was a position I'd earned on my own merit, applying for and progressing through the process without even mentioning it to Robbie. It was important for me to earn this one since I'd been the product of nepotism in some way or another ever since I graduated with my BA in marketing. I'd bounced around from job to job, granted to me by one family friend or another, never quite finding my niche. Finally, though, I'd settled into my career trajectory and homed in my focus. That settling led to an opportunity and I went for it. On the way to meet my brother and sister in law for a celebratory dinner, some idiot ran a red light, destroying our car and my dad's legs. I blessedly walked away with nary a physical scratch, but the emotional ones were enough to damn near destroy me every time I think of how my dad's life had changed for the worst since that day.

We were hopeful at first, as he'd had some semblance of feeling in his lower half immediately after the accident, but while in surgery the doctors discovered that the injury to his spine had been more detrimental that the initial x-rays and scans had picked up. It was a long, dark road back for daddy, filled with a lot of anger and resentment, but he never unloaded any of that onto me.

He was insistent that I not burden myself with his care, but I didn't see it as burden at all. I abandoned my apartment and moved back into our family home, using part of my signing bonus to make some adjustments to the house to make it more accessible for my father to be able to maneuver without impediment. JJ and Robbie were there, to help pick up the slack—emotionally and financially, but I was hellbent on proving that I could do it all myself. That lasted for about six months before I burned out, but luckily my siblings were there to pick up the pieces. I was back to being my dad's primary care provider, with help from a nursing service that was on call, but after this time in New York I was about to be faced with a pretty difficult decision that I needed to consult JJ and Robbie on.

Q4: JANUARY

I was trying to wait for him to wake up, but as I laid next to Nigel watching the steady rise and fall of his chest as he slept, it was getting harder and harder for me to keep my hands to myself. He'd flown in late last night, on a redeye, simply because I'd asked him to come. I was due to be out in New York in a week, but I was craving him, desperate for his presence. We'd been doing this long-distance thing since my last time in NYC and it had been... trying to say the least. I was not a patient woman. I didn't like not getting my way when I wanted or needed something...or in this case someone, and this relationship, as infantile as it was so far had taught me so much with regard to honoring the natural progression of time instead of forcing my will or way. Right now, though, patience was going to be damned because I needed my man.

I ran a hand down his chest lightly, until I reached his waist where the comforter was bunched around him. I'd kicked the covers completely off of myself at some point during the night, feeling like I was in the middle of an incinerator despite it being the dead of winter. I'd completely gotten the cover and sheets off of him and he hadn't stirred, still soundly asleep like I hadn't been low grade molesting him by poking and prodding him for the past twenty minutes. It would honestly be commendable if I wasn't so damned annoyed. That annoyance quickly gave way to unquenchable lust as I realized that he was fully nude beneath the covers and hadn't put on shorts after our final romp and shower last night like I'd thought. I groaned, a wanton, desperate sort of sound and that was the trigger. He opened his eyes slowly, first one lid raising then the other and his gaze focused upon me ready to pounce.

"Aye, were you about to...violate me in my sleep, babe?" he curled into himself, feigning vulnerability and I couldn't help but laugh.

"I...um...well...good morning," I said, leaning down and pressing my lips to his, kissing him deeply as I straddled his thighs.

I pulled back to remove the tee I'd thrown on during one of the six times I got up to use the bathroom over the course of the night.

"I take that as a yes," Nigel groaned once my hands wrapped around him, stroking him to life, then sliding down.

I rocked back and forth in a slow rhythm steadily gaining speed and sighing in relief at the pleasure that coursed through my veins at the simple connection of our bodies. I braced my hands against Nigel's chest, as he laced his hands together behind his head.

"Fine, take it then," he said, petulantly, "it's yours, anyway."

"Oh my god, I cannot believe you."

My rhythm was completely interrupted as I broke down into laughter at his silly ass and collapsed onto his chest. Nigel kept moving, wrapping his arms around my body for leverage as he thrust upward into me.

"And I can't believe you, woman. Damn, the dick is that good that you had to just try and take it?"

I burrowed my face deeper into his neck, feeling my face grow hot at his line of questioning. Of course, my embarrassment just made him go even harder. Nigel's hands trailed down my back, latching onto my ass as he began thrusting upward into me even harder.

"Answer the question, baby," he crooned between strokes, "is the dick that good or nah?"

I was helpless to do much more than moan as he caught a rhythm that I instinctively began ride, rolling my hips against him in measured waves.

"Yeah, that shit must be *real good* to you. Can't even form an answer to a simple question," Nigel growled, speeding up his strokes driving more powerfully into me.

Each stroke drew a sharp cry of varying pitches from me. I couldn't even form proper words, just estimations of syllables as tears streamed from my eyes. The sensations of his hands gripping my ass tightly combined and his dick feeling as if it was destroying my walls in the best of ways drove me insane. Both were insanely overwhelming, sending me into a tailspin. I gave up even trying to keep up, dissipating into a writhing pile of ecstasy atop Nigel. That didn't deter him at all as he reversed our positions, hooking my legs over his shoulders. Staying on his knees, he was thrusting at a downward angle that felt like he'd unlocked a new level in my pussy with the way my legs began quivering uncontrollably and I screamed my throat raw as I tumbled into orgasm. Nigel wasn't far behind me, releasing into me with a roar that I felt more than heard as his body collapsed onto mine. After a few moments he withdrew from me, settling onto his side and looking at me with humor in his eyes.

"What?" I asked.

"See why we couldn't just stay at your people's house? A man can't even try to rest peacefully with his woman coercing him into sex. You happy, you got ya lil orgasm now? Can I go back to bed?"

I peeked over his shoulder to take a look at the clock, "Yes, you can sleep for a couple more hours. Then...we can go on that little...um...errand I wanted to take you on, remember?

Nigel smirked before pulling my face into his for a lazy lip lock, "Sounds good to me, love."

No sooner than the words left his mouth, Nigel had already fallen into a light slumber, a snore sounding off into the relative quiet of the room. I shook my head in disbelief as I got up out of the bed to go use the restroom and start getting ready for the day. I needed a little time to mentally prepare for the afternoon. After I showered and dressed, I sat on the couch in the suite, watching tv until I fortified myself enough to wake Nigel up to get him going on our journey. I guess all that fortification led me to slumber as I found myself being jostled awake by Nigel hunkered down in front of me, shaking my shoulder.

I sat up, rubbing my eyes, "What time is it?"

"Quarter of two," Nigel replied, catching me by the arm as I shot up in alarm, "I know you probably didn't want to sleep that long, but I remembered you saying that we just needed to get to wherever we're going between two-thirty and three so, I hope this is enough time for us to still make your window. You just looked so...completely at ease that I didn't wanna wake you, beautiful."

I'd been having some trouble sleeping lately, so I definitely appreciated his forethought and honestly it didn't matter what time we went to where we were going. I got up, rewashed my face, grabbed my large tote bag that I'd thankfully packed before I fell asleep, and pulled Nigel out of the room as I ordered a Lyft. I hadn't told him where we were going on purpose but when we rounded the corner that would put us directly in front of the wrought iron gates that housed our destination, I knew I had to spill the beans.

"So, I know you think you've met everyone in my fam, but I have one more very important person that you need to meet too," I said, as the Uber stopped in front of the Riverwoods Cemetery, the final place my mother was laid to rest.

If he was shocked, Nigel didn't it be known, instead he simply clutched my extended hand as I led him onto the winding cobblestone path at the cemetery's entrance. We walked along silently until I stopped near a tree and I turned to speak to Nigel.

"Ok, so...I'm gonna need you to wait right here. I need to speak to Mama privately first, and then I'll wave you over, okay?"

Nigel nodded once and I took off across the grass, stopping three rows from where I'd left him standing by the tree. Despite it being winter, it was inexplicably warmer than usual, with the temps hovering in the mid 40s, so it was brisk out, but not unbearably so. But I'd been out here every year on the day we lost her, and I wasn't going to let this January twenty-second pass without me finding myself out here. That was why I'd so desperately needed Nigel because I didn't want another one to pass without him being out here with me. I dug into my bag to pull out the wool blanket I always laid out in front of her gravestone on my visit. I cozied right up to the smooth black marble, rubbing a hand against the laser etched version of her face on the surface.

"Hey, mama. Whew, so girl...a lot has happened since I've come out here to talk to you last. I don't even know...where to begin. Well I guess I should start with the biggest news. I've met somebody mama and...honestly, he kinda seems too good to be true, but I'm riding it out. He's so handsome, and smart, and most importantly kind, Ma. The man will contort himself into a pretzel bending over backwards to make sure I'm good and...you know as well as I do that, I don't have much experience with this whole thing, but I am in deep mama. I love this man so much that my heart is almost overwhelmed, you know? I guess that's a good thing, yeah? So, I brought him here, to meet you. And I know you already fussing about why I hadn't brought him out here while we're courting and all that...but I wanted to be sure and mama, I'm more than sure."

I turned around to wave Nigel over. He moved swiftly, but still with that swagger that was his brand of unique cool. He eased down on the blanket next to me, pulling me in close.

"Nigel, meet my mama, Josephine Lewis. Mama, meet the love of my life, Nigel Cook."

Nigel extended his arms, resting one hand upon the top of my mother's gravestone and wrapping the other arm around me, "Pleased to meet you Miss Josephine. I've heard so much about you."

* * *

"Anybody ever told you that you worry too much, kid?" my big brother said, flopping down on the couch beside me and throwing an arm around my shoulder.

"Or...do you not worry enough, mister *everything is gonna be fine I got this*!" I grumbled.

"You really finna be all up in this new year with antagonistic energy on ya spirit, lil sis? That's not good for your root chaka khan or whatever the hell it is that Rob be talking about when she's laid out on the couch with her ears full of ambient whatever from that *What's Going Om* app."

"Root...chaka...khan. I swear to God, mommy must've dropped you on the head at least ten times when you were a baby, JJ," I laughed.

"Ten?" a rough voice grumbled from the edge of the room, "more like forty. God rest her soul but me and Josie ain't know nothing about no babies when your brother come along. That boy stayed rolling off a bed, table, couch, wherever we placed him. We didn't get no reports from down at the school that he needed extra help, so we figured those bumps just knocked some rightful sense into him."

JJ and I both laughed at that. I loved when Daddy shared memories of my mom since mine were very fuzzy around the edges, since I'd been a preteen when she passed. Lately though, I'd been missing her now more than ever; *needing* her presence as an extra reassurance that everything really was going to be all right. Daddy and JJ were good for some of that, but there's just nothing like a mother's calming presence to recenter her child's frantic spiraling. My life was in complete upheaval right now, all my own doing and I was equal parts nervous and excited for all that was to come.

"I was sent in here to let y'all know brunch is finally done," my dad said, wheeling his way further into the room, "Got me running errands like a damn town crier."

He grumbled, but I knew he was secretly pleased about it. One of my dad's new favorite things was assisting Robyn in the kitchen when she was preparing big meals. It'd started when he moved in with them around Thanksgiving and continued on throughout the rest of the holiday season. He called himself her sous chef, donning a hat and chef's coat and looking damned adorable whilst doing so. I wouldn't dare tell him just how adorable he looked though because I didn't wanna hear his mouth about how there were many words that I could use to refer to a grown ass man, but adorable wasn't one of them. There was no other word, however, in my vast vocabulary that adequately conveyed the mirth in his eyes as he maneuvered around, pitching in and feeling like his old self again. JJ and Robbie had an open floor concept on the first level of their home, so it made Daddy's tooling around much easier than it was in our house. Well, our *former* house. It had officially sold on the first of December, cementing the start of a new era in all of our lives.

"I'm gonna wait for Nigel to get back," I said, not getting up from the couch and following my dad and brother toward the dining room.

"He woulda been here if somebody didn't send him outside for some nonsense. It's coffee in there," JJ teased, "you too good for Folgers now."

"Hush, Jaren," Robyn fussed, "You know she's off of caffeine for her little fast or whatever."

"That's right, sis! Defend my baby's honor," Nigel chuckled, coming through the door and heading straight toward me with a large cup from *Perk*, "One pumpkin spiced crème, milady."

"Damn, you are laying it on kinda thick bro, she already wearing the ring," JJ joked, "You won. None of this extra shit is necessary at all."

Nigel had seamlessly integrated into the family, with Daddy instantly adopting him as a son and him and JJ bonding instantly over shared hatred for the same sports teams. It was wild to know that what was initially supposed to be a one-night stand turned into me finding a love that I never knew my life was missing. When he got down on one knee in front of my entire family on Christmas Eve, I didn't have a second thought as I screamed yes before the question had left his mouth completely. We'd moved quickly, but at not one juncture of our courtship did this not feel...*prophetically right*.

I got up from the couch trailing Nigel into the dining area, "You are such a hater. You could learn a little something from my sugabooga about showing your lady she's valued."

"Sugabooga," JJ cried, incredulously, "Fam, please tell me you ain't going out like that."

Nigel looked down at me, shaking his head, "That's gonna be a no from me, babe."

I giggled, knowing the ridiculous nickname would draw that exact response. I'd been teasing him over the past few months with outrageous nicknames since he complained that my insistence on calling him Nigel was giving him a complex. I wasn't big on the cutesy name calling though. He was more than deserving, considering the major shift in our relationship over the past three months. We did Thanksgiving with his folks out in Brooklyn, and I had been so anxious about meeting his extended family. None of those fears were valid in any way as his sister and their cousins, welcomed me in the moment I crossed the threshold of his Aunt Bonnie's house. They kept me hemmed up in the kitchen with the aunts as they finished up the preparation of dinner. I brought a sweet potato bourbon pound cake with me that was also a major hit. Before we left, the family's matriarch told me not to come back to any further family gatherings without that cake. Suffice it to say, that one statement allayed any feelings of insecurity I'd had up until that moment.

"Ugh, fine, I'll keep trying," I fake whined.

Nigel lowered his head to speak directly into my ear, teasingly whispering, "Or you could just give in to the zaddy wave like the rest of the girls."

I reared back, "Rest of the girls?"

"Whoa whoa, relax killa, I meant girls in general not any damn girl that I know personally."

"That's what I thought," I sassed, smirking before I brought his hand to rest upon my abdomen, "besides, I think this little one will have the market cornered on calling you daddy."

Nigel's face screwed up in confusion before giving way to a large smile, "No way."

I nodded, feeling the tears cresting in my lower lids and willing them not to fall. I knew that if I spoke a solitary word, I'd completely lose it.

Nigel gently cradled my face, whispering back to me, "You having my baby? Like no bullshit."

"Yep," I replied simply, the last syllable barely out of my mouth before Nigel took it with an urgency that took my breath away.

"Hey man, you gotta stop molesting my sister over this fine breakfast that my wife has made, fam!" JJ cracked.

"Leave 'im alone, Junior," my dad chastised.

He already knew my big news; he was the first one that I'd told my news. After my mother passed, my dad had become a confidant of mine, moving into the space that she'd occupied as one of the closest people on earth to me. I'd had my suspicions when I could barely keep food down at Nigel's folks' house on Thanksgiving, but they weren't confirmed until I'd come back home and visited my doctor. I was equal parts scared and excited, but I'd waited to share the news with Nigel because I'd wanted to get used to the idea that I was going to be a mother. Not carrying this pregnancy to term was never an idea that passed through my mind, but I did have my doubts about how he'd received the news. After all, we were already moving at warp speed. Bringing a damned baby into the mix? That was sure to send us into overdrive. This reaction however, allayed all of my fears. I should have known better than to have anything, but the utmost faith in this man and his commitment to me, our relationship and continual happiness.

"Damn, are they gonna come up for air and share

the good news with us too or nah?" Robyn stage whispered.

That quip was enough to break up the moment Nigel and I were sharing, drawing low laughter from us both. I tried looking somewhat sheepish as we pulled apart, but the way Nigel beamed as he looked down on me in awe just made me grin even harder.

"I just let Nigel know that in about six or so months, he'd have another nickname so he should get off my back about giving him one," I said, giggling at the puzzled look on JJ's face before he figured it out.

"Oh shit! You just had to upstage me and have the first grandchild, huh, baby sis? Sheesh!" he said, getting up and pulling me from my chair to wrap me in a tight hug, pressing a kiss to my cheek, "Congrats, big head."

Robyn was slower to round the table, feigning anger, "First I lose you to corporate and then you go and show me up by getting knocked up first? Wow. All I ever did was love you, Janey."

"Shut up, Robbie!"

"Congrats, Baby Jane," Robyn said, squeezing me tighter, "and don't try to act like you forgot your promise to name your firstborn after me for sending you to NYC to find the love of your life."

"Wait...when did I promise that?"

"Okay, well, technically never," Robyn replied, breaking our embrace, "but it's something the both of you should think about honestly. Robyn is a unisex name. And look at how many talented people carry it —Williams, Fenty, Givens, Wright, Harris, Hood!"

"Did...you just say Robin Hood?" Nigel chuckled.

"What," Robyn replied, shrugging, "fictional or not, that boy name rings bells in these streets."

That set everyone off in laughter before we sat down to dig into the food that Robbie and Daddy made. As we sat eating, laughing, and talking, Nigel would reach over and rest a large palm over my belly, rubbing absently at the bump that had yet to manifest. Every time his palm wandered over to my abdomen, I could not repress the large grin that covered my face. Life right now felt almost too good to be true, but instead of questioning it, I was leaning into the good, readying for the blessings sure to be on the road ahead.

Afterword

If you enjoyed this book, please consider leaving a review on Amazon and/or Goodreads.

Keep up with my podcast #FallsonLove at:
www.nicolefalls.com
Follow me on Twitter:
www.twitter.com/_nicolefalls
Follow me on Instagram:
http://www.instagram.com/_nicolefalls
Like me on Facebook:
https://www.facebook.com/AuthorNicoleFalls
Join my Facebook Group:
https://www.facebook.com/groups/NicsNook/

About the Author

Nicole Falls is a contemporary Black romance writer who firmly believes in the power of Black love stories being told. She's also a ceramic mug and lapel pin enthusiast who cannot function without her wireless Beats constantly blaring music. When Nicole isn't writing, she spends her time singing off key to her Tidal and/or Spotify playlists while drinking coffee and/or cocktails! She currently resides in the suburbs of Chicago.

Also by Nicole Falls

Accidentally in Love Series:

Adore You

Smitten

Then Came You

Holliday Sisters Series:

Noelle the First

Brave Hearts

Started From A Selfie

The Illumination of Ginger

Standalone Titles

Sparks Fly

Last First Kiss

sugar butter flour love

All I Want for Christmas

A Natural Transition

Lessons in love series (collaboration with Bailey west and Té russ)

Road to Love

Distinguished Gentleman Series (anthology collection organized by book euphoria)

Switched at Bid

Nymphs and trojans Series (collaboration with Alexandra warren)

Shots not fired

Made in the USA
Middletown, DE
22 September 2022

10673661R00047